Aesop's Fables

Rewritten by Gwen Petreman

Illustrated by Chris Stone

Each fable has been rewritten at 3 different reading levels

Aesop's Fables

Rewritten by Gwen Petreman

Illustrated by Chris Stone

Each fable has been rewritten at 3 different reading levels

This book is dedicated to Dan Petreman, Jeff Petreman

& Michelle (Petreman) Nickel

Thanks to Joseph Mancuso and Erich Jacoby-Hawkins for their contributions

Order this book online at www.trafford.com
or email orders@trafford.com

Most Trafford titles are also available at major online book retailers.

Illustrated by Chris Stone.

Printed in the United States of America.

ISBN: 978-1-4269-3673-9 (sc)
ISBN: 978-1-4269-3674-6 (e)

Trafford rev. 12/16/2010

 www.trafford.com

North America & international
toll-free: 1 888 232 4444 (USA & Canada)
phone: 250 383 6864 ♦ fax: 812 355 4082

About Aesop

It is believed that Aesop lived in ancient Greece about 600 years B.C. He was a slave who loved to tell stories. One of his masters was so impressed with his story-telling that he freed him. Even kings welcomed him to their courts to tell his stories.

It is believed that his stories may have come from all over the world as well as from earlier times.

His fables mostly featured animals that acted like humans and were able to talk to each other and to humans.

Many of the lessons we find in his fables are often quoted by people when facing a variety of situations in today's world. Perhaps one of the most quoted lessons by parents and teachers is the one from The Grasshopper and the Ants.

Rationale for Rewriting Aesop's Fables

Although Aesop's fables have been rewritten many times by a variety of authors over the years, Aesop's fables have never been specifically rewritten to address the variety of reading levels found in all primary classrooms. Therefore, each fable has here been rewritten at three different levels. These fables are ideal for classroom teachers, resource teachers and parents who home-school.

Visit www.gwenpetreman.com.

Table of Contents

The Blue Heron

The Blue Heron -Version 1

Long, long ago in a far away land there lived a blue heron.

One day he was hungry.

He began to look for fish to eat.

He began to look for fish in the river.

He saw a fish.

He looked at the fish.

He said, "A little fish like that is not big enough for a heron like me!"

Next he saw another fish.

He cried, "I don't even want to open my big beak for a small fish like that!"

Soon he saw a bigger fish.

He still wanted something bigger and better.

He let the third fish swim away too.

He waited and waited for a bigger fish to swim by.

He did not see another fish.

He waited for a bigger fish the whole afternoon!

He finally saw a tiny snail.

By this time he was very hungry.

He was now quite glad to eat the tiny snail!

The lesson: Never be too fussy or you may end up getting very little or nothing at all.

The Blue Heron -Version 2

Long, long ago in a far away land there lived a blue heron.

One day he was extremely hungry.

He decided that he wanted a huge fish to eat.

He began searching in the river for a big fish.

Soon he saw a fish.

He declared, "That fish may be fine for a kingfisher, but it is simply not fit for a heron like me!"

A little while later he spied another fish.

He cried, "I can't even be bothered to open my beautiful beak for anything that small!"

Soon he noticed another fish that was even bigger than the other two.

He was still not satisfied and he let the third fish escape.

He waited patiently for a larger fish.

He waited the whole afternoon, but to avoid the blazing sun, the fish had disappeared into the cool depths of the river.

He finally found a teeny snail.

By this time he was starving!

Feeling quite foolish he greedily devoured the very tiny snail.

The lesson: Never be too fussy or you may end up getting very little or nothing at all.

The Blue Heron -Version 3

Many centuries ago, in a distant country, there lived a blue heron.

One day when he felt famished he decided to journey to a nearby river in search of a large, succulent fish.

When he arrived at the meandering river he immediately noticed a fish.

He declared, "A handsome heron like me should not have to eat an insignificant little fish like that!"

A few minutes later he spied another fish.

He sneered, "I can't even be bothered wasting my time opening my beak for another undersized fish!"

Soon he spotted a third fish that was larger than the other two.

He was still not satisfied with this ordinary fish and he let the third fish escape.

He waited the whole afternoon, but to avoid the blazing sun, all the fish had vanished into the cool depths of the river.

After much searching he finally found a tiny snail.

By this time he was so hungry and weak he almost collapsed in the mud.

Feeling quite foolish he quickly devoured the teeny-weeny snail.

The lesson: Never be too fussy or you may end up getting very little or nothing at all.

The Boy Who Cried Wolf

The Boy Who Cried Wolf -Version 1

A long, long time ago there lived a boy.

The boy looked after sheep.

One day he was bored.

Then he got an idea.

"Help! Help! Help! Help! Help! Help!

A wolf is coming! A wolf is coming!" he cried.

The men in the town ran to help the boy.

They ran fast. They ran very fast.

"Ha! Ha! Ha!" laughed the boy.

"I tricked you! I tricked you! Ha! Ha! Ha!"

A few days later the boy got bored again.

Once again he yelled, "Help! Help! Help!

The wolf is coming! The wolf is coming!"

Once again the men ran fast to the boy.

Once again the boy laughed, "Ha! Ha! Ha!

I tricked you! I tricked you!"

The men went back home. They were very, very angry.

A few days later a wolf did come to eat the sheep.

"Help! Help! Help!" yelled the boy. "A wolf is coming!"

"It's that silly boy trying to trick us again!" said the men from town.

No one came to help the boy.

The wolf ate almost all of the sheep.

The lesson: If you keep on telling lies, no one will believe you when you tell the truth.

The Boy Who Cried Wolf - Version 2

A long, long time ago in a far away land there lived a boy.

His job was to look after the sheep.

Sometimes looking after the sheep was very boring.

Suddenly he had what he thought was a great idea.

"A wolf is coming! A wolf is coming!" he shouted.

"The wolf's going to snatch the sheep!

Help! Help! Help!" he shouted.

The men in the town came running as fast as they could.

"Ha! Ha! Ha!" laughed the boy, "I tricked you!"

The men were furious!

A few days later the boy got bored again.

Once again he shouted, "Help! Help! Help!

The wolf is coming! It's almost here!"

Once again the men ran very quickly to the boy.

Once again the boy laughed, "Ha! Ha! Ha! I tricked you!"

The men stomped back to the village.

They were disgusted with the boy's trickery.

A few days later a hungry wolf spied the sheep.

"Help! Help!" shouted the boy. "A wolf is coming!"

The men glanced at each other and cried,

"It's that silly boy trying to trick us again!"

"Help! Help! Help! Please help!" screamed the boy.

No one came to help the boy.

The wolf ate almost all of the sheep.

The lesson: If you keep on telling lies, no one will believe you when you tell the truth.

The Boy Who Cried Wolf - Version 3

Many centuries ago, in a distant country, there lived a boy.

His job was to keep the sheep safe from wild animals.

Sometimes, when nothing exciting happened, tending to the sheep could be really boring.

One day he was extremely bored.

Suddenly, he had what he thought was a brilliant idea.

"Help! Help! A wolf is coming! A wolf is coming!

The wolf is attacking my sheep right now!" he screamed.

"Help! Help! Help!" he shouted repeatedly.

Some men in the town quickly raced to the field where the shepherd boy was calling for help.

When they finally arrived at the pasture the boy started laughing uncontrollably, "Ha! Ha! Ha! I tricked you!"

The busy men were furious! "Don't you ever pull a stunt like that again!" they warned him.

The shepherd boy very quickly forgot the men's warning.

A few days later, he got bored again.

Once more he yelled loudly at the top of his lungs,

"Help! Help! The wolf is killing the sheep!"

For a second time, some men raced to the meadow.

Once again the boy laughed loudly, "Ha! Ha! I tricked you!"

The men were angrier than before!

A few days later a hungry predator came to the pasture looking for prey. It was the wolf!

The boy was terrified! He let out the loudest yell he could muster, "Help! Help! The wolf is here! It's eating my sheep!"

The men refused to be tricked a third time, so they ignored the boy's cries.

The wolf devoured sheep after sheep until he was unable to eat another bite.

The lesson: If you keep on telling lies, no one will believe you when you tell the truth.

The Boys and the Frogs

The Boys and the Frogs -Version 1

A long, long time ago there lived two boys.

One day they went down to the pond to play.

The boys started to throw stones.

The boys threw the stones into the pond.

They tried to make the stones skip on top of the water.

They laughed and laughed when the stones

skipped on top of the water.

Three frogs poked their heads out of the water, "Please,

please do not throw stones in the pond!"

"But why not? We are having so much fun!" they cried.

"Well we're not having any fun at all!" croaked the frogs.

The lesson: Make sure when you are having fun, that your fun is not bothering others!

The Boys and the Frogs -Version 2

A long, long time ago there lived two boys in a far away land.

They loved to play all kinds of games by the pond.

One day they ventured down to the pond to have some fun.

The boys started to throw stones recklessly into the pond.

They tried to make the stones skip on top of the water.

The stones flew in all directions across the smooth water.

The boys were having lots of fun.

They laughed and jumped with excitement when the stones

skipped on top of the water.

Finally, some angry frogs poked their heads out of the

water and croaked, "Please, stop throwing those stones!"

"But why?" cried the boys. "We are having so much fun!"

"Well we're not having any fun at all!" croaked the frogs.

> *The lesson: Make sure when you are having fun, that your fun is not bothering others!*

The Boys and the Frogs -Version 3

Many centuries ago, in a distant country, there lived two boys.

The boys' favorite pastime was to play down by the pond.

One day the boys decided to throw pebbles across the water.

They laughed uncontrollably when they managed to get the

flat pebbles to skip across the pond's smooth surface.

They were so thrilled by their successful attempts at skipping

their stones across the water that they threw dozens and

dozens of pebbles across the pond.

Finally, some frustrated frogs poked their heads out of the

water and croaked, "Please stop throwing those stones!"

"But why?" cried the boys. "We are having so much fun!"

"Well we're not having any fun at all!" croaked the frogs.

The lesson: Make sure when you are having fun, that your fun is not bothering others!

The Peacock and the Crane

The Peacock and the Crane -Version 1

A long time ago there lived a peacock and a crane.

The peacock liked to brag.

"Look at my feathers! They are so beautiful!

Look at your feathers! They are gray as dust!"

The crane did not like the peacock's mean words.

But the crane did not say anything to the peacock.

Instead the crane spread her wings.

She flapped her wings and flew up into the sky.

"Follow me!" cried the crane.

The peacock tried to fly.

He tried and tried and tried.

But he simply could not fly!

☾

The lesson: Being useful is more important than being beautiful.

The Peacock and the Crane - Version 2

A long time ago there lived a peacock and a crane.

The arrogant peacock was always bragging to the crane.

"Look at my colorful feathers! They are simply stunning!

Look at your dull feathers! They are as gray as dust!"

cried the vain peacock.

The crane remained silent. She spoke not a single word.

Then the crane spread her powerful wings and soared up

into the blue sky.

"FOLLOW ME!" the crane shouted back to the peacock.

The peacock tried to flap his wings. He tried again and

again. But he simply could not fly!

☾ ☾

The lesson: Being useful is more important than being beautiful.

The Peacock and the Crane -Version 3

Many centuries ago there lived a peacock and a crane.

The peacock was constantly ridiculing the crane.

"I hope you noticed that I have the most stunning

feathers in the world," bragged the peacock.

The peacock sneered, "Your feathers are colorless and

ordinary! They are as gray as dust!"

The crane remained silent. She ignored the peacock's daily ridicule.

Then one day she spread her magnificent wings and

soared up into the distant sky.

"FOLLOW ME!" the crane shouted loudly to the peacock.

The peacock frantically flapped his wings. He flapped and flapped

until he finally collapsed from exhaustion.

No matter how hard he tried he simply could not fly!

☾ ☾ ☾

The lesson: Being useful is more important than being beautiful.

The Crow and the Pitcher

The Crow and the Pitcher -Version 1

A long, long time ago in a far away land there lived a crow.

One day the crow was thirsty.

She was very, very thirsty.

She looked and looked for some water.

Finally, she found some water.

It was in the bottom of a tall pitcher.

The crow tried and tried to reach the water.

She could not reach the water.

She became very, very thirsty.

"Oh no! I think I will die from thirst," cried the crow.

All at once she thought of a clever plan.

She dropped one pebble into the water.

She kept on dropping more and more pebbles.

As she dropped the pebbles into the pitcher the water rose higher and higher.

Finally, the crow could reach in for a cool drink of water.

> The lesson: When you want something badly enough you will probably figure out a way to get it.

The Crow and the Pitcher -Version 2

A long time ago in a far away land there lived a crow.

One day the crow became very thirsty.

Her mouth felt very dry.

She started to look for some water.

She became quite excited when she finally found some water.

The water was in the bottom of a tall pitcher.

The crow tried, without any luck, to reach the water from the bottom of the pitcher.

Her throat felt like it was going to crack.

"Oh no!" she cried. "If I don't get a drink at once I will die!"

Suddenly she thought of a clever plan.

She quickly dropped one pebble into the water.

Then she dropped half a dozen pebbles into the pitcher.

As she dropped the pebbles into the pitcher, the water rose upwards towards the brim of the pitcher.

Finally, the water rose so high that the crow could easily reach into the pitcher and enjoy a cool, refreshing drink.

ॐ ॐ

> *The lesson: When you want something badly enough you will probably figure out a way to get it.*

The Crow and the Pitcher -Version 3

Many centuries ago, in a far away country, there lived a crow.

One day the crow became parched with thirst.

Her mouth felt dry like sawdust.

She began flying across the sky in search of water.

She became quite excited when she finally found some water.

Unfortunately, the water was at the bottom of a tall pitcher.

The frustrated crow tried again and again to reach the water at the bottom of the pitcher.

Suddenly, a clever idea popped into her head.

She quickly picked up a pebble and dropped it into the water.

She continued to drop pebble after pebble into the pitcher.

As each pebble plopped in, the water started to rise slowly toward the brim of the pitcher.

Finally, the water rose so high that the crow could easily plunge her beak into the pitcher.

She finally was able to quench her thirst with a cool, refreshing drink of water.

ༀ ༀ ༀ

The lesson: Necessity is the mother of invention.

The Dog and the Donkey

The Dog and the Donkey - Version 1

A long, long time ago there lived a dog and a donkey.

The dog's owner was always petting the dog.

The dog's owner gave him treats.

Every day the dog jumped on the owner.

Every day the dog licked the owner's face.

The donkey became jealous.

The donkey decided to act just like the dog.

The donkey ran into the house.

The donkey raced around the house like a dog.

He broke the owner's dishes!

The donkey tried to jump on the owner.

He tried to lick his face.

The poor owner tumbled to the floor.

The owner was furious!

~

The lesson: Do not try to act like someone else. Be yourself.

The Dog and the Donkey - Version 2

A long, long time ago there lived a dog and a donkey.

The dog's owner spent many hours petting his beloved dog.

At the end of the day the dog always received treats.

When the owner came home from work the dog jumped up and licked his face.

The donkey became extremely jealous.

The donkey decided to act just like the dog.

When the owner arrived home from work the donkey raced around the house just like a dog.

He smashed most of the owner's dishes.

Then, the donkey decided to jump on the owner.

Next, he attempted to lick the owner's face.

The poor owner tumbled backwards onto the floor.

The owner was furious with the donkey.

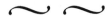

The lesson: Do not try to act like someone else. Be yourself.

The Dog and the Donkey - Version 3

Many centuries ago there lived a dog and a donkey.

The dog's owner spent countless hours petting his faithful dog.

When the owner returned home from work his beloved dog raced

to the front door, leaped up and licked his master's face.

The man pampered the dog with his favorite treats.

In time, the donkey became extremely envious of all the affection

and attention that the dog received from his master.

The donkey foolishly made the decision to behave just like the dog.

When the man arrived home from work the donkey raced

wildly and excitedly around the house.

Unfortunately, most of the man's dishes crashed to the floor.

Next, the donkey jumped on the man and licked his face.

The astonished man tumbled backwards onto the floor banging

his head on the wall. He was furious!

The lesson: Do not try to act like someone else. Be yourself.

The Dog and the Oyster

The Dog and the Oyster - Version 1

A long, long time ago there lived a dog.

The dog loved to eat.

He loved to eat eggs.

He ate eggs every day.

He ate eggs from the henhouse every day.

He began to eat the eggs whole.

One day the dog saw something on the beach.

It looked like an egg.

He thought it must be an egg.

He gulped down the egg.

The dog got a terrible tummy ache.

He moaned and groaned, "Oh no! Not all round things are eggs!"

((

The lesson: If you act in too much of a hurry, you might regret your actions.

The Dog and the Oyster - Version 2

A long, long time ago there lived a dog.

The dog loved to eat raw eggs.

He devoured eggs morning, noon, and night.

He ate eggs from the henhouse every day.

The dog got so greedy he ate the eggs whole!

One day the dog spied something on the beach.

Instantly, he decided it must be an egg.

But it was not an egg, it was an oyster.

In one quick gulp the dog swallowed the oyster whole.

The dog got a terrible stomachache.

He moaned and groaned, "I guess not all round things are eggs!"

((

The lesson: If you act in too much of a hurry, you might regret your actions.

The Dog and the Oyster - Version 3

Many centuries ago, in a far away country, there lived a dog.

This silly dog was crazy about raw eggs.

He thought eggs were the most delicious things he had ever tasted.

Every day he sneaked into the henhouse and snatched all the eggs!

This dog became so obsessed with eggs that he began to eat them whole!

One day the dog spied something oval-shaped on the beach.

He thought to himself this must be a delicious egg.

With his tail wagging, he raced toward the object.

In one quick gulp the dog swallowed the object.

Then the dog got a terrible stomachache.

In his rush he had swallowed an oyster and not an egg!

(((

The lesson: If you act in too much of a hurry, you might regret your actions.

The Dogs and the Hides

The Dogs and the Hides - Version 1

A long, long time ago there lived some dogs.

One day the dogs were very hungry.

They found some bones and hides.

The bones and hides were in a stream.

They tried to grab the bones and hides.

They tried and tried, but they could not reach them.

They decided to try to drink the stream dry.

They drank and drank and drank.

They drank and drank some more.

The water in the stream stayed the same.

They finally fell to the ground.

They were too full to drink any more!

The lesson: Never try to do something that you know is impossible!

The Dogs and the Hides - Version 2

A long, long time ago there lived some dogs.

When they could find no food they became extremely hungry.

Luckily, they found some old bones and wrinkled hides.

They discovered them in a winding stream.

They immediately tried to snatch the bones and hides.

They made many attempts at grabbing the bones and hides.

After a noisy meeting they came up with what they thought was

a brilliant solution.

They decided to drink up all the water in the stream.

After slurping up water as quickly as possible for a long time,

they discovered to their frustration that the water remained

exactly the same.

The lesson: Never try to do something that you know is impossible!

The Dogs and the Hides - Version 3

Many centuries ago, in a distant country, there lived some dogs.

After going without food for several days, the dogs became extremely hungry.

Luckily, one day they discovered some sun-bleached bones and weather-beaten hides in a nearby stream.

They immediately attempted to snatch the bones.

They tried many times to grab the hides and bones, but all their attempts were futile.

After a lengthy meeting with much arguing, they decided to drink up all the water in the stream.

They started to slurp up the water as quickly as they could.

Their stomachs got so full they were ready to burst!

They continued to drink at a frantic pace, but the water level in the stream remained exactly the same!

At last they collapsed on the ground totally exhausted!

ૐ ૐ ૐ

The lesson: Never try to do something that you know is impossible!

The Fox and the Crow

The Fox and the Crow - Version 1

A long time ago there lived a fox.

One day he went for a walk. He saw a crow in a tree.

The crow had a piece of cheese in her mouth.

The fox wanted the cheese.

"Wow! Your feathers are so beautiful!" said the

fox to the crow.

"I bet your voice is beautiful too," said the fox.

"I would love to hear you sing!" he said.

The crow opened her mouth to sing.

The cheese fell right down into the fox's mouth.

"Ha! Ha! Ha!" laughed the fox as he ran away with the

cheese.

The lesson: Don't be tricked by someone who flatters you because they want something from you.

The Fox and the Crow - Version 2

Long ago a fox spied a crow on a tree branch.

The fox noticed the crow had some cheese in her beak.

The fox was hungry and wanted the cheese.

"Wow! What beautiful feathers you have!" cried the

fox to the crow.

"Your feathers are so shiny and shimmery," he cried.

"I bet your voice is beautiful too. I would love to hear you

sing!" declared the sneaky fox.

The happy crow opened her mouth to sing.

The cheese tumbled right down into the fox's open mouth.

"Ha! Ha! Ha!" laughed the tricky fox as he quickly hurried

away with the crow's cheese.

> *The lesson: Don't be tricked by someone who flatters you because they want something from you.*

The Fox and the Crow - Version 3

Many centuries ago a cunning fox was going for a stroll.

He spied a crow sitting on a gnarled branch of a tree.

The fox noticed that the crow had an enormous piece of creamy

cheese in her mouth.

The fox's mouth started to drool. He wanted the cheese for himself.

"Wow! What beautiful and shiny feathers you have!" declared the

sneaky fox.

"Your feathers look like ebony sparkling in the sun," he cried.

"I bet your voice is sweet and mellow," exclaimed the fox.

"I would love to hear you sing!" declared the fox.

The crow was so flattered by the fox's compliments that she

opened her mouth wide to sing.

Her cheese quickly tumbled down into the fox's open mouth.

"Ha! Ha! Ha!" laughed the fox, as he devoured the cheese.

> The lesson: Don't be tricked by someone who flatters
> you because they want something from you.

The Fox and the Goat

The Fox and the Goat - Version 1

A long, long time ago there lived a fox and a goat.

One day the fox fell. He fell into a well.

The well was very deep.

The fox tried and tried to get out.

He could not get out. Soon a goat came by.

"I'm thirsty," said the goat.

The fox said, "Jump in and have a drink!"

The goat jumped into the well. At once the fox jumped on

the goat's back and out of the well.

The goat finished drinking the water. He tried and tried to

get out of the well. But he could not get out of the well.

The goat called and called for the fox, but he was long gone.

The lesson: Look before you leap!

The Fox and the Goat - Version 2

A long time ago there lived a fox and a goat.

One day the fox tumbled into a deep well.

The fox tried frantically to get out.

Soon a thirsty goat came wandering by.

The goat asked the fox if the water was fresh and clean.

The fox replied, "The water in here is fabulous!

Jump in and have a refreshing drink!"

Quickly the goat jumped into the well. In a flash the fox

leapt on the goat's back and out of the well.

After the goat had quenched his thirst he soon

realized that he could not get out of the well.

He called and called for the fox, but he was long gone.

> *The lesson: Look before you leap!*

The Fox and the Goat - Version 3

Many centuries ago, in a distant land, there lived a fox.

One day the fox tumbled into an extremely deep well.

He immediately struggled to get out of the well. After numerous

unsuccessful attempts, he fell down exhausted.

Soon a very thirsty goat came wandering by the well.

The goat peered into the well. "Is the water down there

fresh and clean?" asked the thirsty goat.

The fox replied, "The water down here is wonderful.

Come on down and get yourself a refreshing drink."

The goat leapt down into the well and the fox jumped on

the unsuspecting goat's back and out of the deep well.

After the goat had finished drinking he slowly

realized that he could not get out of the well!

He called for the cunning fox, but he was long gone.

The lesson: Look before you leap!

The Fox and the Leopard

The Fox and the Leopard - Version 1

A long, long time ago there lived a fox and a leopard.

The leopard was very proud of his coat with spots.

He kept bragging to the fox.

"I have the most beautiful coat in the world!"

he bragged.

"Your coat is plain," said the leopard to the fox.

The fox looked at the leopard, but he said nothing.

The leopard got angry.

Finally, the fox said, "You have a beautiful coat.

But you don't have a beautiful mind.

I think it's better to have a beautiful mind."

The lesson: Looking beautiful, does not always
mean that you have a beautiful mind.

The Fox and the Leopard - Version 2

A long, long time ago there lived a fox and a leopard.

The leopard thought his coat was beautiful!

The leopard was very proud of his coat with spots.

He was always bragging to the fox about his coat.

"I have the most beautiful coat in the world!

Your coat is plain. You have no spots! How boring!"

said the leopard to the fox.

The fox just looked at the leopard, but he said nothing.

The leopard started to lose his temper.

Finally, the fox said, "You may have a beautiful coat,

but I don't think you have a beautiful mind.

I think it's better to have a beautiful mind.

That is what I call real beauty!"

🦋 🦋

> *The lesson: Looking beautiful does not always*
> *mean that you have a beautiful mind.*

The Fox and the Leopard - Version 3

Many centuries ago there lived a fox and a leopard.

The leopard thought that his coat was extremely beautiful.

He thought that his coat was especially attractive because of

its spots. He was continuously bragging.

"My coat is the most beautiful in the world!" he boasted.

"I can't believe how plain and ugly your coat is. A coat without

spots is just so boring!" the leopard cried.

The fox stared at the leopard, but he didn't utter a single word!

The fox's silence infuriated the leopard.

Finally, the fox spoke up, "You may have a beautiful coat,

but I don't think you have a beautiful mind. I think a beautiful mind is

always superior to a beautiful coat!

That is what I call real beauty!"

❧ ❧ ❧

The lesson: Looking beautiful does not always
mean that you have a beautiful mind.

The Fox and the Stork

The Fox and the Stork - Version 1

A long, long time ago there lived a fox and a stork.

One day the fox asked the stork to come for lunch.

The fox gave the stork some soup in a flat dish.

The stork could not eat the soup with her long beak.

The fox laughed at the stork. The stork did not get angry.

She asked the fox to come to her house for lunch.

The stork gave the fox soup too.

She gave the fox soup in a very tall jar.

The fox could not reach the soup.

The fox got angry. He growled and growled at the stork.

"Why are you angry?" asked the stork.

"I did not get angry when you played a mean trick on me!"

> *The lesson: Do not play tricks on your friends,*
> *unless you can stand the same tricks yourself.*

The Fox and the Stork - Version 2

A long, long time ago there lived a fox and a stork.

The sly fox enjoyed playing tricks on his friends.

The fox gave the stork some soup in a very flat dish.

The poor stork couldn't eat the soup with her long beak.

The fox laughed and laughed at the hungry stork.

The stork did not lose her temper.

She kindly invited the fox to come to her house for lunch.

The easy-going stork decided that she too would make soup.

The soup was inside a very tall and narrow jar.

All the fox could do was lick the outside of the tall jar.

The furious fox growled loudly. The stork asked, "Why are you

angry? I did not get angry when you played a mean trick on me!"

> *The lesson: Do not play tricks on your friends,*
> *unless you can stand the same tricks yourself.*

The Fox and the Stork - Version 3

Many centuries ago, in a distant land, there lived a fox and a stork.

The sly fox continually played tricks on the stork.

The fox loved to poke fun at the stork's long beak.

One day the sneaky fox invited the unsuspecting stork for lunch.

He gave the stork vegetable soup in a flat dish.

The fox roared with laughter when the stork attempted to eat the soup.

All the frustrated stork could do was wet the tip of her long beak.

However, the stork stayed calm. She didn't lose her temper.

She very politely invited the fox to her house for lunch.

The stork also decided to give soup to the sly fox.

She poured the soup into a very tall jar with an extremely narrow neck.

All the fox could do was lick droplets from the outside of the jar.

The fox didn't remain calm like the stork had. He snarled and growled.

The stork stared at the fox and responded very quietly, "Why are you so

angry? I did not lose my temper when you played a mean trick on me!"

The lesson: Do not play tricks on your friends,
unless you can stand the same tricks yourself.

The Goose and the Golden Eggs

Gwen Petreman

The Goose and the Golden Eggs - Version 1

A long, long time ago there lived an old farmer.

The old farmer had some geese.

One goose was special.

This special goose laid golden eggs!

The special goose laid a golden egg every day.

The farmer sold the golden eggs.

The farmer sold the golden eggs at the market.

Soon he became rich. He became very rich.

He also became greedy. He became very greedy.

He wanted all the golden eggs at once.

He got his axe. He got his sharp axe.

He cut open the goose. He looked inside, but he didn't find a

single golden egg!

The lesson: If you become too greedy, you might lose everything you already have.

The Goose and the Golden Eggs - Version 2

A long time ago, in a far away land, there lived an old farmer.

He had a flock of geese. One of the geese was special.

This special goose was able to lay eggs which were solid gold.

The goose laid a golden egg every single day.

The happy farmer sold the golden eggs at the local market.

In no time at all he became very rich.

After a while he became extremely greedy and impatient.

He wanted every single golden egg immediately.

He got his sharp axe and killed the goose.

He couldn't believe his eyes when he looked inside the goose.

He didn't find a single golden egg!

The lesson: If you become too greedy, you might lose everything you already have.

The Goose and the Golden Eggs - Version 3

Many centuries ago there lived an old farmer.

He had a gaggle of geese, a gander and some goslings.

One of the geese was unique. She laid golden eggs!

This amazing goose laid a golden egg every single day.

The ecstatic farmer sold the golden eggs for huge sums of money.

In no time at all he became extremely wealthy.

At the same time, he also became exceedingly impatient and greedy.

He wasn't satisfied with getting just a single egg every day.

He was determined to get all the golden eggs immediately.

He got his sharp axe and slaughtered the goose.

He couldn't believe what he saw when he looked inside the

cavity of the goose.

He didn't find a single golden egg!

The lesson: If you become too greedy, you might lose everything you already have.

The Grasshopper and the Ants

The Grasshopper and the Ants - Version 1

A long time ago there lived a grasshopper and some ants.

The grasshopper loved to play.

He just played and played and played all summer.

The ants worked and worked and worked.

They worked all summer getting food for the winter.

The grasshopper said, "Come and play with me!"

The ants said, "No! No! No!"

The grasshopper played and played and played.

Soon fall came. Snow covered the ground.

All winter long the ants ate and ate their food.

The grasshopper had no food to eat.

He wished that he had worked all summer instead of

playing.

The lesson: First do all your work and then you play.

The Grasshopper and the Ants - Version 2

A long time ago there lived a grasshopper and some ants.

The grasshopper's favorite pastime was to play.

The ants who lived nearby loved to play too.

But they knew it was necessary to prepare for the long, cold winter.

The grasshopper cried, "Stop working! Come and play in the sun!"

The ants replied, "We need to gather food while it is plentiful."

The grasshopper could only think about relaxing and playing.

The sun was shining brightly and he wanted to enjoy every minute of it.

Soon autumn arrived.

The leaves on the trees were turning red, orange and yellow.

A few months later the snow began to fall.

In no time at all the green grass was covered with a white blanket of snow.

The ants had plenty of food to last them right through the whole winter.

The hungry grasshopper searched for food everywhere.

He now wished that he had listened to the good advice from the ants.

> *The lesson: First do all your work and then you play.*

The Grasshopper and the Ants - Version 3

Many centuries ago there lived a grasshopper and some ants.

The grasshopper's favorite pastime was to play.

The ants who lived nearby loved to play too.

But the ants believed in being prepared for the winter.

They knew it would be necessary for them to labor long hours in

order for them to accumulate enough food to survive the long, harsh winter.

The grasshopper cried, "Stop working! Come and enjoy the summer!"

The ants replied, "We do not want to die of starvation in the

winter. We must gather food while it is plentiful."

The grasshopper refused to worry about the upcoming winter. The sun was

shining brightly and he wanted to enjoy every minute of it.

Soon autumn arrived. The leaves on the deciduous trees were turning scarlet,

orange and yellow. A few months later the snow started to fall.

In no time at all the grass was completely covered with a blanket of snow.

The ants had a huge supply of food to last them right through the whole winter.

Sadly, the grasshopper searched for food in the snow. He now wished that

he had collected his food first and played after all the work was done.

> The lesson: First do all your work and then you play.

The Greedy Dog

The Greedy Dog - Version 1

A long, long time ago there lived a dog.

One day he found a bone. It was a big, big bone.

He ran home with his big bone.

Soon he came to a wide river.

He looked into the river.

He saw another dog in the river.

The dog in the river had a big bone too!

He dropped his big bone.

He jumped into the river to grab the other big bone.

As soon as he jumped into the river the other dog was gone!

The dog had to swim and swim to get to the other side.

When the dog got to the other side he realized

how foolish he had been.

❧

The lesson: It is very foolish to be greedy.

The Greedy Dog - Version 2

A long, long time ago there lived a dog.

One day a butcher gave him a big bone.

The dog hurried home with his bone.

On the way home he had to cross a long bridge.

He looked into the river where he saw another dog

with a huge bone.

He dropped his own bone and jumped into the river

to get the huge bone from the other dog in the river.

As soon as he jumped in, the other dog disappeared.

The dog had to swim very quickly to reach the other

side of the swirling river.

When the dog reached the other side he realized

how foolish he had been.

❧ ❧

The lesson: It is very foolish to be greedy.

The Greedy Dog - Version 3

Many centuries ago, in a distant country, there lived a dog.

One day a kind butcher gave him an enormous bone.

The delighted dog quickly raced home with his bone.

On the way home he had to cross a wide, winding river.

As he hurried across the bridge, he noticed another dog in the swirling waters of the river.

He couldn't believe his eyes when he discovered that the dog in the river had a huge bone clenched in his teeth.

His greed consumed him and he immediately dropped his own bone and leapt into the river to steal the enormous bone.

His intention was to quickly grab the bone from the other dog and immediately race away with both bones.

When he jumped into the river the other dog disappeared.

When the dog reached the other side he realized how foolish he had been.

∾ ∾ ∾

The lesson: It is very foolish to be greedy.

The Lion and the Mouse

The Lion and the Mouse - Version 1

A long, long time ago there lived a lion.

One day he was sleeping.

A little mouse ran across the lion's paw.

The lion grabbed the little mouse.

The lion roared, "I am going to eat you!"

The little mouse cried, "Please, please let me go!

Someday, I'll help you!"

"Ha! Ha! Ha!" laughed the lion. "You are too little to help me! But I

will let you go this time."

A few days later the lion got caught in a net.

"Help! Help! Help!" he roared loudly.

The mouse found the lion caught in a hunter's net.

The mouse chewed and chewed on the net.

Soon the lion became free. He jumped out of the net.

"Thank you! Thank you!" the lion roared as he ran away.

The lesson: Even if you are small you can still help someone who is big.

The Lion and the Mouse - Version 2

A long, long time ago there lived a lion.

One day a small mouse raced across the lion's paw.

The lion quickly grabbed the mouse and roared, "I'm going to

gobble you up!"

"Please let me go and someday I'll help you," cried the mouse.

"Ha! Ha!" roared the lion with laughter. "How do you think a

tiny mouse like you can possibly help a powerful lion like me?"

But he let the mouse go free.

A few days later the lion got tangled up in some rope.

"Help! Help! Help!" he roared loudly. The mouse heard the

lion's roar and he immediately started running.

He discovered the poor lion caught in a hunter's net.

He quickly began gnawing at the net and finally freed the lion.

"Thank you! Thank you!" roared the lion as he hurried away.

The lesson: Even if you are small you can still help someone who is big.

The Lion and the Mouse - Version 3

Many centuries ago, in a distant country, there lived a fierce lion.

One day he was sleeping soundly among some tall grasses.

A timid mouse scurried across the lion's paw.

The lion grabbed the mouse and roared, "I'm going to devour you!"

The terrified mouse cried, "Please release me and someday I'll help you."

The fierce lion roared with laughter. "You can't be serious. How can a little pipsqueak like you possibly help me? But, you seem like a decent little fellow, so I will release you!"

A few days later the lion got tangled up in a hunter's net.

The tiny mouse could hear the lion's desperate cries for help.

The mouse raced like the wind in the direction of the loud roars.

The mouse very quickly began gnawing at the hunter's net.

Just as the hunters were returning the lion leapt free.

"Thank you! Thank you!" roared the lion as he swiftly raced away.

The lesson: Even if you are small you can still help someone who is big.

The Old Lion and the Fox

The Old Lion and the Fox - Version 1

A long, long time ago there lived an old lion.

The lion was very old. He was too old to catch food.

He pretended that he was very sick.

He lay down in his cave.

As animals came to visit the old lion, he ate every single one

of them!

One day a fox came to visit the old lion.

The lion said, "Please-please come inside. I'm so sick!

I'm too sick to get up."

The fox said, "I don't want to. I see animal footprints

going into your cave, but none coming out. Did you eat

all the animals that came to visit you?"

The lion didn't know what to say.

The lesson: Learn from the mistakes of others.

The Old Lion and the Fox - Version 2

A long, long time ago there lived an old lion.

The lion was too frail to catch his own food.

He decided to pretend that he was ill.

He lay quietly in his cave and waited for visitors.

When the animals came one by one to visit him, the

old lion pounced on them and devoured them.

One day the fox came by for a visit.

The lion said to the fox in a weak voice, "Please-

please step inside. I'm too weak and old to get up."

The fox replied, "I don't think I want to. I noticed all

kinds of animal footprints going into your cave, but

none coming out. What happened to all those animals?

Did you eat them?" The lion didn't know what to say.

$\sim \sim$

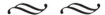

The lesson: Learn from the mistakes of others.

The Old Lion and the Fox - Version 3

Many centuries ago, in a distant country, there lived a lion and a fox.

The lion was getting old and quite feeble. He was too

weak to venture out of his den to catch his prey. He

decided to pretend that he was too sick to move.

When the other animals came to visit the lion, he swiftly reached out

and snatched them with his sharp claws and devoured them.

Now he had plenty to eat without having to leave his cozy cave.

One day a fox decided to see how the sickly lion was feeling.

When the fox came within reach of the cave the lion cried, "Please Mr.

Fox, step inside my cave as I'm too weak and sick to come out."

The fox was a very observant animal and he replied, "No thank you

Mr. Lion. I have no desire to enter your cave. I noticed all kinds of

footprints going into your cave, but I don't see any footprints

coming out of your cave! What happened to all those

animals? Did you eat them?"

The lion didn't utter a single word.

The lesson: Learn from the mistakes of others.

The Snake and the Eagle

The Snake and the Eagle - Version 1

A long time ago there lived a snake and an eagle.

One day the snake saw the eagle.

The snake grabbed the eagle.

The eagle tried and tried to get away.

A man saw the eagle. He helped the eagle get away.

The snake was mad. He was very mad.

He tried to bite the man. The snake's poison went

into the man's drinking horn.

Soon the man went to get a drink from his horn.

The eagle grabbed the horn.

He hid it away from the man.

The lesson: If you are kind to someone, they will probably be kind to you.

The Snake and the Eagle - Version 2

A long, long time ago there lived a snake and an eagle.

One day the snake grabbed the eagle.

The eagle frantically tried to get away.

A man saw the poor eagle and felt sorry for it.

He rescued the eagle. The snake was furious.

He tried to bite the man. The snake missed and the poison

from the snake's fangs entered the man's drinking horn.

Minutes later the man decided to get a drink from his horn.

Suddenly, there was a rushing of wings.

The eagle grabbed the horn with the poisonous water

and hid it far away.

The lesson: If you are kind to someone, they will probably be kind to you.

The Snake and the Eagle - Version 3

Many centuries ago there lived a snake and an eagle.

One day the venomous snake grabbed the unsuspecting eagle.

The terrified eagle tried desperately to escape from the snake.

A wanderer hiking through the country spied the poor eagle.

He managed to rescue the eagle. The snake was furious!

Swiftly the snake swung his head toward the man and attempted

to plunge his fangs into the man. Fortunately, he missed! The

poison from his fangs penetrated the man's drinking horn.

A short while later the man became very thirsty. He proceeded

to get a drink from his horn.

Suddenly, he heard a rushing of wings. It was the grateful eagle.

The eagle grabbed the horn with the poisonous water and

dropped it into the valley below.

The lesson: If you are kind to someone, they will probably be kind to you.

The Tortoise and the Hare

Gwen Petreman

The Tortoise and the Hare - Version 1

A long time ago there lived a tortoise and a hare.

The hare could run really fast. The tortoise was slow.

"Let's have a race!" cried the hare.

The race began. The hare ran and ran really fast.

The tortoise plodded along very slowly.

The hare was so far ahead he lay down for a nap.

The hare slept and slept and slept.

The tortoise walked and walked and walked.

The hare woke up. He raced as fast as he could.

The hare was too late. The tortoise won the race.

All the animals cheered and cheered and cheered.

The lesson: Never give up. Always keep on trying to reach your goal.

The Tortoise and the Hare - Version 2

A long time ago there lived a tortoise and a hare.

The hare was an amazing runner. The tortoise was

extremely slow. The hare constantly bragged to all the animals,

The hare sneered at the tortoise, "You are so-o-o slow!"

All the animals urged the hare and tortoise to have a race.

The hare laughed loudly, "You must be kidding! I can beat the

tortoise running backwards! He's slower than a snail!"

The race began. The hare took off like a shooting star.

Half way to the finish line the hare decided to have a short nap.

While the hare snoozed, the determined tortoise never slowed down.

When the tortoise had almost reached the finish line the hare

woke up. The hare took off like a shot from a cannon. But he

was too late! The animals cheered wildly as the tortoise trudged

across the finish line!

The lesson: Always keep on trying to reach your goal.

The Tortoise and the Hare - Version 3

Many centuries ago, in a distant land, there lived a tortoise and a hare.

The hare was swift like the wind. He could run extremely fast.

The tortoise always plodded along very slowly. He was extremely slow. The

hare was very arrogant. He was constantly bragging. From dawn until

dusk, he would boast loudly about his amazing speed.

"I guess everyone has figured out by now, that I am simply the

fastest animal in the whole wide world!" boasted the annoying hare.

The hare sneered at the tortoise, "You are unbelievably slow!

There is no doubt that you are the slowest animal in the whole world!"

The other animals got totally fed up with the hare's loud bragging.

They had a quick meeting. They decided that the tortoise should

challenge the hare to a race. When the hare heard about the challenge

he could barely contain his laughter. He laughed so hard that he

collapsed on the grass.

"I have never heard anything so ridiculous!" declared the hare.

A few days later the other animals organized the race.

"Get ready! Get set! Go!"

"Eat my dust!" shouted the hare as he took off like a shot from a cannon.

The tortoise started off very slowly.

In no time at all the hare had raced so far in front that the tortoise had disappeared from sight.

The hare decided to lie down in the thicket and have a short snooze.

While the hare snoozed, the tortoise kept plodding along.

After he had trudged along for quite a while, the tortoise could see the finish line in the distance.

After a long while the hare woke up with a start. He rubbed his eyes and looked around for the tortoise. He was nowhere in sight!

The hare bounded off so fast he thought his lungs would burst.

He ran faster than he had ever run in his whole life!

He could not believe his eyes when he finally reached the finish line.

There he saw the jubilant tortoise surrounded by an enormous crowd of cheering animals.

The hare never again bragged to his friends that he was the fastest animal in the whole world.

The lesson: Always keep on trying to reach your goal.

Two Friends and a Bear

Two Friends and a Bear - Version 1

Two friends were going for a walk.

A big bear started to chase them!

One friend quickly climbed a tree.

The other friend threw himself on the ground.

He pretended to be dead.

The bear sniffed and sniffed him.

Then the bear walked away.

His friend climbed down from the tree.

He said, "I am so glad the bear did not hurt you.

You are my best friend!"

His friend said, "You climbed up a tree and left me!

I don't want you to be my friend!"

The lesson: A true friend is someone you can count on when you are in trouble.

Two Friends and a Bear - Version 2

Two friends were hiking through the woods.

Suddenly a big bear appeared in front of them!

One friend quickly scrambled up a tree.

The other friend threw himself on the ground.

He lay as quiet as a mouse pretending to be dead.

The bear sniffed him and then lumbered away.

His friend climbed down from the tree.

"I am so glad you are alive. You will always be my

best friend," he beamed.

His friend replied, "I don't think I want someone as a

friend who deserted me when there was real danger!"

The lesson: A true friend is someone you can count on when you are in trouble.

Two Friends and a Bear - Version 3

Many centuries ago, in a distant land, two really good

friends were hiking through the woods.

Suddenly a ferocious bear appeared in front of them!

The two friends froze with terror! Without a word one of the

friends swiftly scrambled up a nearby tree.

The other friend immediately threw himself on the ground.

Like an opossum he pretended to be dead.

With his eyes closed, he barely dared to breathe.

Slowly the bear lumbered over to where he lay motionless on the ground.

The bear sniffed him and then slowly plodded away.

Immediately, his friend climbed down from the nearby tree.

"You're alive! You'll be my best friend forever!" he cried.

His friend replied, "I don't think I want someone as a friend

who abandoned me when there was real danger!"

❀ ❀ ❀

The lesson: A true friend is someone you can count on when you are in trouble.

CPSIA information can be obtained
at www.ICGtesting.com
Printed in the USA
LVHW03s1510030718
582556LV00001B/4/P